ISBN 1-56163-205-8

Printed in Hong Kong

5 4 3 2 1

Ken wishes to thank the following people who helped in various ways in producing this book:
Technical advice: Ken Oyer, Sean Cavanaugh and Martin Satryb.
Models: Tonni Pidgeon (Gustav), Elizabeth Pauko (McBride), Sabrina Fox (Maya), Garth Fox (Barlow), Mona Meyer (Emma), Fritz Brecke (Johnson), Sharon Mayer (Trayner), Eric Peterson (Hodgson), Carrie Flowers (Yates), Bruce Huff (Popolski), Ken Bauer (Fraser), Brian Michael 'Boom-Boom' Bendis (Mikey), and Gustav Klimt (himself).
Bolstering of ego: Dan Brereton, Brian Michael Bendis, David Mack, Joe Pruett, and Malcolm Bourne.
Support and patience: Mona and Riley Meyer.

A Mad Hatter Studios International Production
Created\Written by **Malcolm Bourne**
Created\Visualized\Lettered by **Ken Meyer Jr.**

NANTIER · BEALL · MINOUSTCHINE
Publishing inc.
new york

YES, HOLD THE LINE PLEASE..
MCBRIDE FOR YOU, MR. G...
...I DON'T KNOW, DARLIN'...
...REALLY COULD USE YOUR HELP...

McBride
...I KNOW I SAID I WOULDN'T ASK AGAIN...
...WORRIED WE'RE OUT OF OUR DEPTH...

Gustav
P.I.
PARANORMAL
INVESTIGATOR
SQUISH

IN
THE CASE OF THE
BLOODLESS
POLITICIAN

CHAPTER ONE

THE AYES HAVE IT BY 323 VOTES TO 276; I DECLARE THE MOTION CARRIED.

I THOUGHT THAT MIGHT BE CLOSER.

NO, JUST ANOTHER BORING EVENING SESSION. FANCY A PINT, GRAHAM?

NOT *TONIGHT*. HOT DATE AT THE CLUB.

TAXI!

WHAT DO YOU TELL JANET?

I TELL HER NOTHING. THAT'S THE *BEAUTY* OF A FLAT IN LONDON AND A HOUSE IN THE COUNTRY...

WHERE TO, UH...MR. *BAIRSTOW*, IS IT?

THE STRAND. THE DOMINO.

YES, GUV. GENTLEMAN'S CLUB, ISN'T IT?

JUST *DRIVE*. I'M NOT IN THE MOOD FOR A *CHAT*.

SPEAK TO THE LADY IN CHARGE...

...SORRY, LUV. CAN'T HELP IT IF THE GIRLS ARE ILL. BUT THERE'S A SPECIAL ***NEW*** ATTRACTION TONIGHT...

SHE'D ***BETTER*** BE SPECIAL, EMMA. AND I EXPECT A ***DISCOUNT***.

...OF COURSE, OF COURSE!

THIS WAY, MR. B...

MAKE YOURSELF COMFORTABLE. MAYA WILL JOIN YOU.

...PEOPLE ARE CRAZY ENOUGH TO GO JOGGING AT 4 A.M... HELPED US FIND HIM EARLIER, MA'AM.

HAS ANYONE TOUCHED HIM YET?
NO, MA'AM. WE WERE WAITING FOR YOU.
I SHOULD HOPE SO.
THAT'S ODD. THERE'S NO BLOOD.

PROBABLY 'CAUSE THE GUY WAS BROUGHT HERE FROM SOME-WHERES ELSE, JUDGING FROM THE TRAMPLED BUSH.
STICK TO WAITING, UH, CLARKSON.

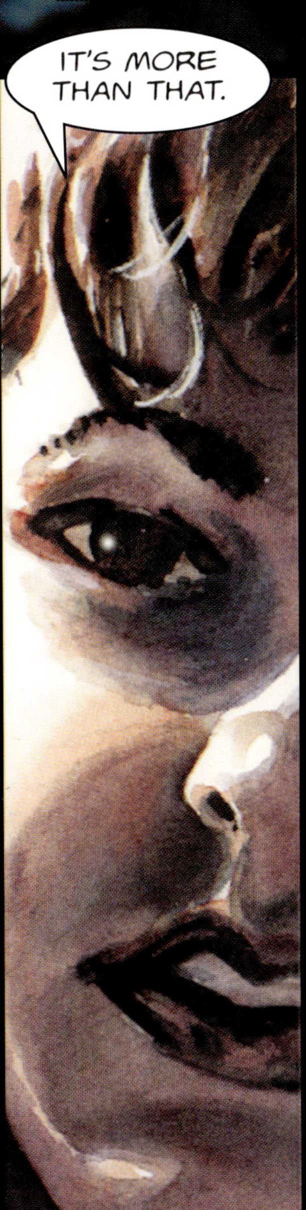
IT'S MORE THAN THAT.

POLICE POLICE
OK, I'M TURNING HIM-

-OVER.
OH MY G-KAFF KAFFF
YOU KNOW WHO THIS IS, DON'T YOU? MR. FAMILY VALUES, THE HONOURABLE MEMBER OF PARLIAMENT FOR HAMSTEAD GARDEN, GRAHAM BARLOW.
THE PRESS ARE GOING TO HAVE A FIELD DAY WITH THIS ONE...

London Sun
Was this woman JFK's secret bride?
Exclusive: RICHARD KAY reveals a bitter row over bills for their Caribbean holiday
WHY

Sun
Bendis Found!
his woman ecret bride?
HARD KAY reveals a bitter for their Caribbean holiday
Exclusive
M.P. Murdered in Kinky Sex Killing

OK, YOU LOT, TIME TO GET TO WORK. BARLOW IS NUMBER FOUR.
London Sun
Bendis Found!
Was this woman JFK's secret bride?

TYPICAL. THREE RENT BOYS DIE AND NOBODY *GIVES* A SHIT. THROW A *TORY* INTO THE PICTURE AND-
ENOUGH. A MURDER IS A MURDER AND WE'RE COLLECTING A SERIES OF THEM.
SO IT'S TRUE, ISN'T IT? A SERIAL KILLER AT LARGE?
YES. NOW KEEP QUIET AND LISTEN.
FIRST VICTIM, MARCH 17TH, KING'S CROSS. FOUND IN A LEATHER MASK AND A WHIP. PETER, UH FLETCHER.
SECOND, APRIL 9TH, ALSO AT KING'S CROSS, THE STATION ITSELF, EDDIE FERGUSON.
WE KNOW NUMBER THREE- DUNCAN. SCOTTISH LAD.
AND NOW HE'S GOT SOME EXTRA HOLES, AS YOU CAN SEE.
SO. SOMEBODY'S PLAYING AT VAMPIRES?
HOW D'YOU KNOW THEY'RE ONLY *PLAYING*, JOHNSON?

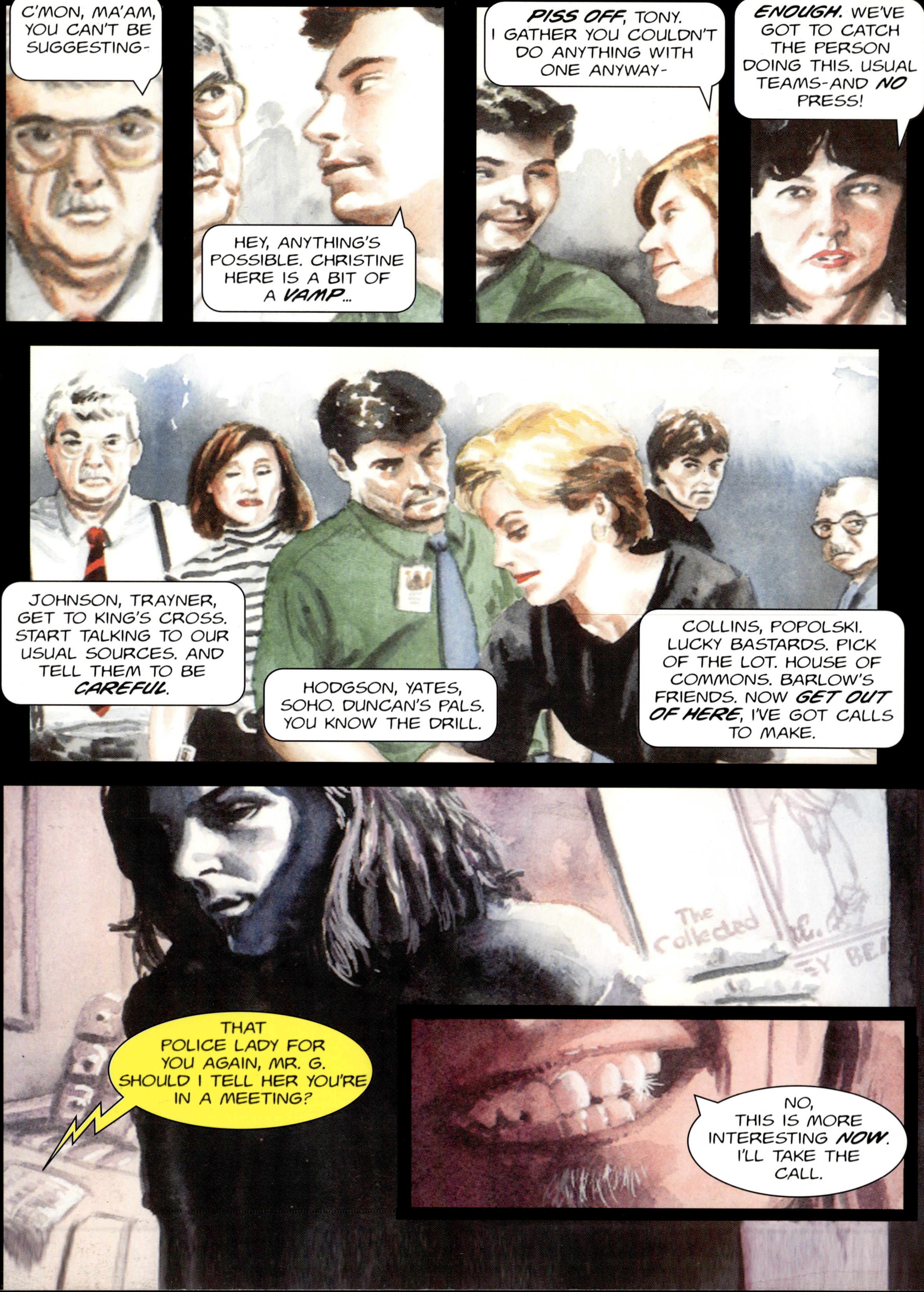

C'MON, MA'AM, YOU CAN'T BE SUGGESTING-

THAT POLICE LADY FOR YOU AGAIN, MR. G. SHOULD I TELL HER YOU'RE IN A MEETING?

NO, THIS IS MORE INTERESTING ***NOW***. I'LL TAKE THE CALL.

CHAPTER TWO

AND NOW YOU KNOW AS MUCH AS WE DO. SO...
SO.
SO YOU THINK THIS MIGHT BE APPROPRIATE TO MY, UH, SPECIALITY.
WELL, JUDGING BY WHAT YOU'VE DONE FOR US IN THE PAST...
...I THINK FOUR DEAD MEN WITH HOLES IN THIER NECKS MIGHT BE RIGHT UP YOUR STREET.
AH.

London Sun
Mack Sought!
Modern Ripper Caught!
Exclusive: Interview with "Paranormal Investigator" who caught the New Jack
THIS IS DIFFERENT. LAST TIME IT WAS *WOMEN*.
YES, BUT WE NEED YOU AGAIN.
I NEED YOU.
OK. I'LL NEED TO SEE THE BODIES.
THAT MIGHT PROVE... DIFFICULT. WALKER STILL DOESN'T LIKE YOU.
I NEED YOU.
AH, THE JEALOUS BOSS. BUT MY DEMAND STANDS.
I NEED YOU.
I NEED YOU.
MAYBE TONIGHT THEN, AFTER HOURS.
GOOD. HOW MANY ON YOUR TEAM?
SIX. YOU CAN MEET THEM IN THE MORNING. THEY'RE DUE AT EIGHT SHARP.
CAN'T. I'M ON THE TELLY THEN. YOU KNOW...
OH, YES. YOU'RE A FAMOUS ART CONNOISSEUR NOW. I FORGOT.
POLICEWOMEN SHOULDN'T FORGET. ONE MORE THING. KEEP THE NECK MARKS FROM THE PAPERS.

"DON'T WORRY, I ALREADY AM."
OI! GILLIAM! HERE EARLY, AREN'T YA? A WORKIN' MAN, ARE YOU NOW?
AHHHH, PISS OFF!
HELLO? EVENING BANNER.
YES, IT'S ME. GOT SOME HOLES TO TELL YOU ABOUT.
OFF THE RECORD, MATE, OF COURSE.
Evening Banner
JACK'S BACK!
NEW YORK
Herald
INTERNATIONAL
Is Japanese Gripped by Gloom. There Is

...NEED TO INTERVIEW SOME OF HIS FRIENDS.
SEE WHAT THEY KNOW.
CERTAINLY SIR, COME IN. THEY'LL BE AT THE-
"-1922 GROUP MEETING."
YOUR ATTENTION PLEASE, LADIES AND GENTLEMEN. I THINK YOU PROBABLY KNOW WHY WE'RE HERE.
NOW SEE HERE, OFFICER-
DON'T FUCK AROUND.
THIS IS NO TIME FOR NICETIES.
YOU KNOW AS WELL AS I DO WHAT HAPPENED TO YOUR MATE BARLOW.
SO UNLESS YOU ALL WANT TO JOIN HIM.

I THINK I MAY BE ABLE TO ASSIST, OFFICER.

HOW FUCKIN' *UNUSUAL*. AN MP WITH BACK-
ALL RIGHT, POPS.

COME WITH US, MR, UH...
FRASER.

ANYTHING ABOUT HIS, UH, SEXUAL, UH...
DON'T WANT JANET TO KNOW, BUT THERE'S THIS CLUB.
AH. SOHO. A FUCK CLUB.
NOT EXACTLY. A PROPER CASINO PLUS... EXTRAS.

WHAT CLUB? WHAT'S IT CALLED?
THE DOMINO, I THINK.

JANET DOESN'T HAVE TO KNOW, DOES SHE?
LET'S HOPE NOT, MR. FRASIER.

PICADILLY CIRCUS
TRY JIMMIE'S.
YEAH, I KNEW DUNCAN.
HEARD WHAT HAPPENED TO HIM.
JIMMIE'S Tattoo Ink Spot
DID YOU DO HIS, UH, Y'KNOW...
COCK RING.
YEAHH, NOTHING ILLEGAL IN *THAT*, IS THERE?
DEPENDS. KNOW ANYTHING ABOUT HIM? ANY ENEMIES?
SURE... ANYTHING IN IT FOR ME?
YEAH!
WE DON'T LOCK YOU UP ON *SANITATION* GROUNDS. *SPILL* WHAT YOU *KNOW!*
HE TRIED IT ON THIS CLUB.
PROPOSING CLIENTS, IF YOU KNOW WHAT I MEAN.
GOT THE MADAME ANGRY.
LOOKS LIKE SOME-ONE'S VISITING THE DOMINO TONIGHT.
I THINK POPS WILL ENJOY *THAT!*

C'MON, MIKEY, WHAT HAPPENED TO PETE?
HE PICKED THE WRONG MARK, THAT'S ALL WE KNOW.
ANY IDEA WHO?
King's Cros
CAN'T SAY. SOMEONE INTO MASKS AND SHIT.
WHO WAS HIS PIMP, MIKE? WHO'S YOURS?
YOU'RE JOKING! IT'S MORE THAN MY LIFE'S WORTH!
RELAX...
WE JUST WANT TO TALK TO HIM.
AGHHK!
KEN, YOU'LL LEAVE MARKS!
SO?!
FAIR ENOUGH. BETTER TELL HIM, MIKEY.
AGKKK, NAME'S DEREK, OR SOMETIMES DENISE.
CROSS-DRESSER WORKS OUT OF THE DOMINO!

...AND THAT'S THE STORY, CHIEF.
OK, BILL. POPS CAN TRY THE CLUB. TELL HIM TO BE CAREFUL.
OUT.

WHY?

YOU'VE AN OVERACTIVE IMAGINATION, GUSTAV.
SO LET'S PUT IT TO BETTER USE BEFORE WALKER FINDS OUT.

WHAT DID YOU- BRIBE THE ATTENDANT?
Name: P. Fletcher
Age: 15
DOD: 9/12/97
SOME- THING LIKE THAT. HE LIKES TO KEEP PHOTOGRAPHS OF HIS, UH, CUSTOMERS.
AH.
LET'S GET TO KNOW THEM, SHALL WE?
MMMM

GUSTAV! WHAT'S HAPPENING?
I CAN'T...
WHAT'S GOING ON?
WAIT. WHICH ONE IS BARLOW?
OVER THERE.

THUMP
AH, MR, UH, GUSTAV, I PRESUME? COINCIDENCE...
Y-YES. THAT'S RIGHT, HERR KLIMT. I'M HERE ABOUT THE POSITION AS A...
"...MODEL."
WELL.
YES, *INDEED.* AND WHAT A *SPLENDID* MODEL YOU'LL BE. AND THIS...THIS IS *MAYA.*

NOW YOU ARE READY FOR A VERY SPECIAL PICTURE-IT WILL BE CALLED "THE KISS"...

...MAYA...
breeeeeeeeebreeeeeee
breeeeeeeeeee-
BLOODY TECHNOLOGY...
MCBRIDE HERE. THIS HAD BETTER BE-
WHAT? OH SHIT...
AND CHRISTINE... YOU'D BETTER INFORM HIS WIFE.
SOUNDS LIKE BAD NEWS.
YES. YES, IT FUCKING IS.

Popolski
Popolski
Popolski
Popolski
Popolski
Popolski
COME ON...
Popolski

CHRISTINE...?
OH GOD...
ALICE...
ALICE...

CHAPTER THREE

COME ON, JACKIE. YOU'VE FACED WORSE.
SHIT SHIT SHIT
I KNOW, BUT THIS IS DIFFERENT...

TIME IS, AS THEY SAY, OF THE ESSENCE HERE. I NEED TO SEE THE BODY.
MAYBE NOT. BUT IF MY SUSPICIONS ARE CORRECT, I NEED TO COME WITH YOU - I ASSUME YOU'RE GOING...?
YOUR BLOODY CALMNESS ISN'T ALWAYS APPRECIATED, GUSTAV.
YES, OF COURSE. HE'S - HE WAS - ONE OF MY OWN.

A SMALL DIVERSION, IF YOU DON'T MIND...?
WHAT THE FUCK ARE YOU PLAYING AT, GUSTAV?

I NEED TO DO SOMETHING IN MY OFFICE...
...TAKE A PICTURE, SO TO SPEAK..

FUCKIN' GET A MOVE ON...

OH POPS...

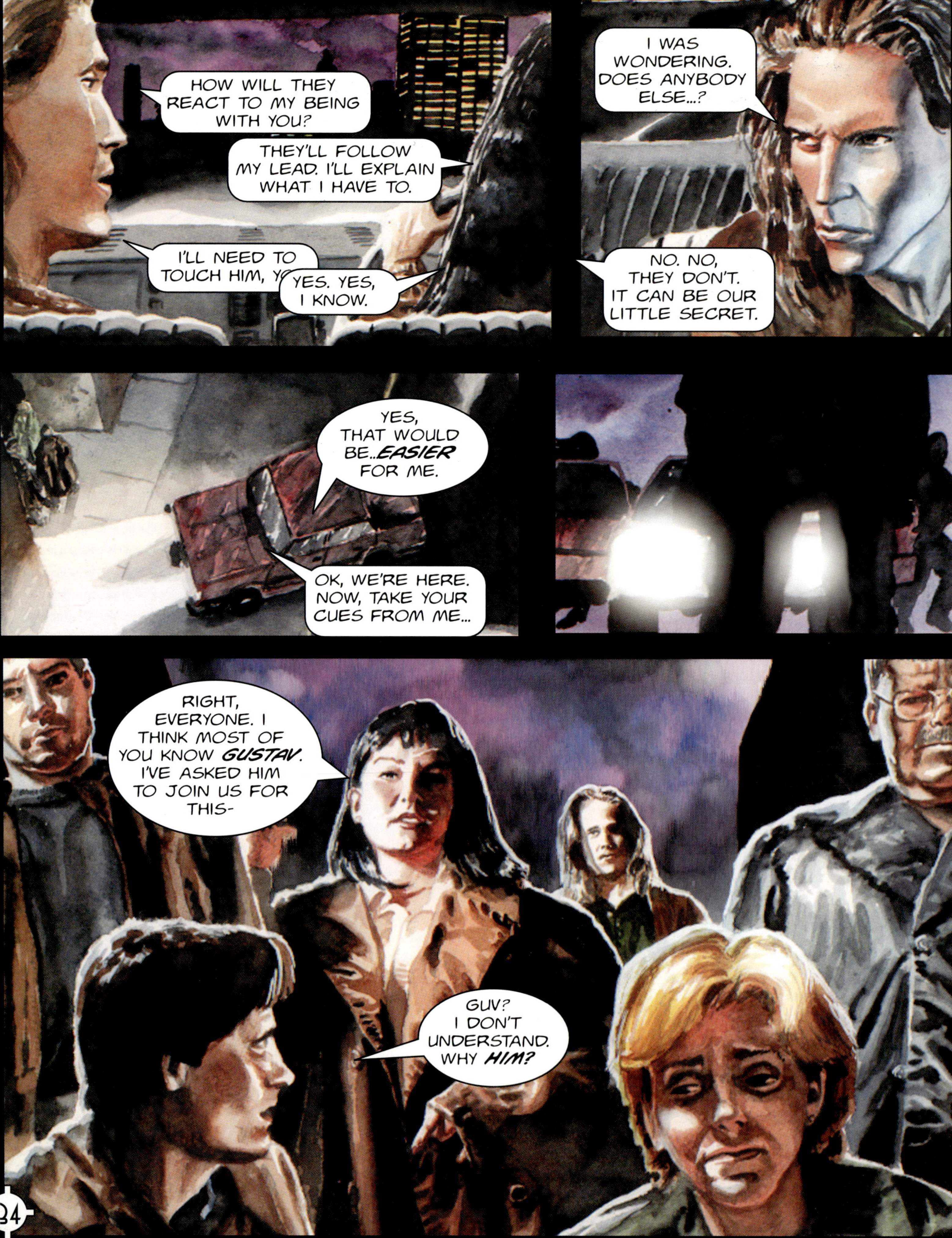

RIGHT, EVERYONE. I THINK MOST OF YOU KNOW *GUSTAV*. I'VE ASKED HIM TO JOIN US FOR THIS-

GUV? I DON'T UNDERSTAND. WHY *HIM?*

C'MON, BILL, THIS IS HARD ENOUGH AS IT IS.
NOW, WHAT'S UP IN THE CLUB?
UH, UNIFORMED OFFICERS ARE INSIDE. NOBODY'S BEEN ALLOWED TO LEAVE.
GOOD. GUSTAV?
THANK YOU. NOW I JUST NEED TO-
WHAT D'YOU THINK YOU'RE-
ENOUGH, COLEEN. LET HIM DO WHAT HE WANTS.

GOOD. YOU CAN REST NOW.
WE'LL CONTINUE TOMORROW.

AND WILL I SEE YOU BEFORE THEN?
UH, NO. I DON'T THINK SO. I THINK I HAVE...

...A PRIOR ENGAGEMENT.

IS HE AS GOOD AS ME?

WH- WHO?
OUR EMPLOYER, HERR *KLIMT*, OF COURSE.
AH, *HIM*.

IT'S FINE, YOU KNOW. FUCKING ANOTHER MAN.
IT'S THE OTHER WOMEN I CAN'T FORGIVE YOU FOR.

LET ME GO-
I DON'T THINK SO
STRONG, AREN'T I?
IT'S ALRIGHT. IT WON'T BE LIKE THOSE WHORES IN LONDON. YOU'LL GET A SECOND CHANCE...
...LOVER.

IT IS AS I FEARED.

WHAT *IS* THIS CRAP?
OK, EVERYONE...

...LISTEN UP. YOU'RE GOING TO HAVE TO TRUST ME ON THIS ONE. AND I TRUST GUSTAV. HE'S HELPED THE FORCE, AND ME, OUT BEFORE.

AND HE'S OUR BEST CHANCE THIS TIME. THIS IS *SERIOUS SHIT* WE'RE STAR-ING AT HERE. POPS SHOULD BE PROOF OF THAT.

GUSTAV IS GOING TO SAY AND DO SOME *STRANGE* THINGS, I EXPECT.

TAKE THEM FROM *HIM* AS YOU WOULD FROM *ME*.

NOW, WE *KNOW* POPS WAS AFTER SOMETHING AT THE DOMINO, DON'T WE? HAS SOMEONE TALKED TO EMMA?
YEAH. SHE DIDN'T KNOW ANYTHING ABOUT DUNCAN, OR ANY *TRANNIE* CALLED DENISE, BUT...
...SHE MENTIONED A *NEW* GIRL. HASN'T BEEN SEEN SINCE BARLOW DIED. COULDN'T FIND ANY PHOTOS OF HER EITHER. NAME OF-

MAYA.

YES. HOW THE FUCK DID *YOU* KNOW?
I KNOW THIS WILL SOUND ODD, BUT SHE'S... WELL...
...A VAMPIRE.

DON'T TAKE THE PISS.
FOR GOD'S SAKE, BILL, DOES HE LOOK LIKE HE'S JOKING?
THINK ABOUT BARLOW'S BODY.
ALL THOSE HOLES.
WHETHER YOU BELIEVE ME OR NOT IS IRRELEVANT. BUT YOU MUST DO AS I SAY.
WHY WOULD SHE COME BACK AT ALL? IF SHE'S REALLY KILLED POPS AND ALL.
SHE MUST. IT'S HER ... SAFE PLACE.
SHE MUST COME BACK TO HER NEST...
...AND TO ME...
RIGHT. WE'LL GO IN ROUND THE FRONT. SHARON, YOU GET THE CORONER TO COME GET POPS.

DON'T KNOW WHAT YOU MEAN! THIS IS A LEGIT-
C'MON, EMMA! WE KNOW SHE WORKS HERE. WE'RE NOT INTERESTED IN YOU!
WELL, MAYBE...

IS THIS HER? IS THIS MAYA?
WHY, THAT'S YOU, MY DEAR! AND YES, I DO BELIEVE THAT'S MAYA, TOO. THAT'S A PAINTING, ISN'T IT...?

TAKE ME TO HER, UH ROOM.
I DUNNO-
DO AS HE SAYS, EMMA.

NOW! QUICKLY!

THIS WAY...
JACKIE, GET YOUR MEN TO EMPTY THE PLACE.
I ONLY WANT YOUR PEOPLE HERE.

I NEED TO BE ON MY OWN FOR THIS BIT, JACKIE. SO MAKE SURE THEY ALL GET OUT OF HER WAY WHEN SHE COMES.

HEY, WATCH IT!
SHUT UP, EMMA.
NOW, GUYS - GET EVERYONE OUT. WE DON'T NEED THEM NOW.

YES, CHRIS, I KNOW IT SEEMS ***BONKERS***, BUT MAC REALLY BELIEVES THIS BLOKE.

AND I THINK I DO TOO. YOU REMEMBER WHAT BARLOW LOOKED LIKE.

AND I DON'T THINK POPS IS MUCH BETTER OFF.

HOW'S HIS WIFE?

BLOODY ***AWFUL***. AND I'M NOT MUCH BETTER.
NO, ME NEITHER-

-OH MY ***GOD***-

SHARON? SHARON!

I'VE GOT HER-*AHHHH!*
RRRRRRRRR!
GUSTAV? CAN IT BE *YOU?*
YOU *KNOW* IT IS.

AT LAST! I HAVE BEEN WAITING SO LONG...
I DON'T BELIEVE YOU, MAYA. THE LAST TIME I SAW YOU WAS WHEN YOU MADE ME...LIKE THIS.
WHEN YOU BIT ME.
AND NOW WE CAN BE LOVERS AGAIN-FOREVER...
NO.
THE KILLING MUST STOP.
SSSSSSS
AAAA!
WHAT HAVE YOU DONE?!
I'M KEEPING US ALL SAFE. YOU CANNOT GET OUT, WHILST THE MORTALS CANNOT GET IN.

YES! WE ARE THE SAME, YOU AND I!
NO. MAYBE ONCE, BUT NO LONGER.
I AM SORRY, MAYA.
SO AM I!
HOW...?

YOU...?
YES. ME.
BUT, I- IF-YOU GOT THROUGH THE FLAMES, YOU'RE...
YES. NOW DO WHAT YOU HAVE TO DO.
YES.
YES, I MUST.

...REST OF HER BODY IS A LONG WAY FROM HERE.
SO IT'S TRUE. AT LEAST YOU DIDN'T STUFF IT WITH GARLIC.
NO. THAT WOULD BE SILLY.
YES. HAHHA!
HAHAHAHA!
AND SO...IT ENDS.
FOR NOW!.
FANCY A DRINK AND A BITE TO EAT? I'M BUYING...
A BITE IT IS.
FIN